Butterfly Meadow

Twinkle and the Busy Bee

Come flutter by

Butterfly
Meadow!

Butterfly Meadow

Twinkle and the Busy Bee

by Olivia Moss
illustrated by Helen Turner

SCHOLASTIC INC.

New York Toronto London Auckland Sydney
Mexico City New Delhi Hong Kong Buenos Aires

For Holly Powell, with lots of love

With special thanks to Sue Mongredien

No part of this publication may be reproduced, stored in a retrieval system, or transmitted in any form or by any means, electronic, mechanical, photocopying, recording, or otherwise, without written permission of the publisher. For information regarding permission, write to Working Partners Limited, Stanley House, St. Chad's Place, London, WC1X 9HH, United Kingdom.

ISBN-13: 978-0-545-05461-4
ISBN-10: 0-545-05461-3

Text copyright © 2009 by Working Partners Limited.
Illustrations copyright © 2009 by Scholastic Inc.

All rights reserved. Published by Scholastic Inc., 557 Broadway, New York, NY 10012, by arrangement with Working Partners Limited. Series created by Working Partners Limited, London.

12 11 10 9 8 7 6 5 4 3 2 1   9 10 11 12 13 14/0

Printed in the U.S.A.

First printing, February 2009

Contents

Butterfly Meadow

Twinkle and the Busy Bee

CHAPTER ONE

Mystery in the Meadow

It was a hot, sunny afternoon in Butterfly Meadow. Dazzle had found a comfortable spot on a sunflower with Skipper and Mallow, two of her butterfly friends. She was just drifting into a dream about delicious nectar. . . .

"Hey, you guys! Something's wrong in the meadow."

Dazzle's eyes snapped open. Her friend Twinkle, a colorful peacock butterfly, zipped around the sunflower.

"What's happening?" Dazzle asked. Twinkle was darting around so fast, it made Dazzle's head spin.

Nearby, Mallow fluttered her small white wings. "Is it a mystery?" she asked, flitting into the air. "I love a good mystery!"

Skipper yawned. "Everything looks fine to me," she said, gazing around. "Twinkle, aren't you hot, racing all over the place?"

Twinkle didn't answer. Instead, she zoomed around the sunflower one more time. The bright colors of her wings blurred together as she flew.

"Well?" Dazzle asked. "Aren't you going to tell us what's going on?"

"I'll *show* you," Twinkle replied mysteriously. "Follow me!"

Dazzle stretched out her wings and fluttered toward her friend, with Mallow close behind. "Come on, Skipper," Mallow called back to the holly blue butterfly. "It's not like you to miss out on an adventure."

"OK, I'm coming," Skipper said,

looking sleepy and flapping her pretty blue wings. "Wait up!"

Twinkle led her friends to a thick hedge at the edge of the meadow. She glanced back, then dived down among the leaves. "In here," she called.

Dazzle, Skipper, and Mallow followed Twinkle, dodging branches. It was cooler out of the sun's glare, but some of the

branches had thorns on them. Dazzle fluttered her pale yellow wings carefully.

Just then, Twinkle stopped so suddenly that Dazzle bumped right into her! Skipper skidded into Dazzle, and Mallow tumbled out of the hedge, trying to stop in time.

"Whoa!" Mallow yelped, fluttering her wings to steady herself. "Pileup!"

Dazzle, Twinkle, and Skipper untangled themselves, giggling. "What are we doing in here?" Skipper asked, smoothing her crumpled antennae.

"I'm about to show you," Twinkle replied. She pointed a wing at a cluster of flowers swaying in the grass below the hedge. "There," she said. "See?"

CHAPTER TWO

Help!

Dazzle peered through the leaves, but she didn't notice anything unusual. The long meadow grass was filled with wild poppies, dandelions, and thistles. "What are we looking at?" she whispered.

"I have no idea," Mallow said. "Twinkle, what is this? A guessing game?"

"Just wait," Twinkle told them. "Keep watching."

A grasshopper leaped into the butterflies' hiding place, almost landing right on top of Skipper. "Hey!" she squealed, folding her wings out of his way.

The grasshopper bent its green head low. "I'm sorry," it said, embarrassed. "I've never met any butterflies in here before."

8

"We're solving a mystery," Mallow told the grasshopper.

Twinkle was still gazing out at the flowers. "Look — there it goes again," she said. "*Now* do you see?"

They all stared, even the grasshopper. One of the flowers was vibrating!

"That's only the wind," the grasshopper said with a laugh. "Now, if you'll excuse me, I'd better hop along." With a spring of its back legs, it leaped away.

"There *is* no wind today," Twinkle said thoughtfully. "There's something happening in that flower."

Dazzle and her friends slowly made their way through the hedge until they were level with the flower. They all watched as its red petals began to shake

violently. Dazzle couldn't help wondering what was going on!

A faint buzzing rang in the air, and the flower shook again. Something was inside it! Dazzle glimpsed a small furry body with wings as an insect tumbled out of the flower and plunged to the ground.

Dazzle hid behind Skipper. "What was that?" she whispered.

"I don't know," Skipper replied, leaning out of the hedge for a better look.

"There's only one way to find out," Twinkle decided. "We need to investigate. Come on!"

Dazzle, Twinkle, Skipper, and Mallow flew out of the hedge and hovered above the flowers. Dazzle stayed close to her friends. Who knew what that creature could be?

The grass rustled, and the butterflies heard a faint moaning. "Help me!" came a scared little voice. "Help!"

CHAPTER THREE

Clueless

A small insect with black and yellow furry stripes was rolling around in the grass. It had black legs and two pairs of filmy wings. "It's a bee!" Dazzle said in surprise.

The bee waved its short front legs when it saw Dazzle. "I'm Sting," she said. "Will you please help me?"

Dazzle was
just about to land
beside Sting
when Twinkle
swooped in front
of her. "Be
careful," she
whispered. "You know what bees are
like. They have sharp stingers. She could
hurt you!"

Dazzle looked at Sting, struggling in
the grass. She knew that bees had
stingers, but she couldn't ignore an
insect asking for help. She dodged
Twinkle and flew down to the little bee.
"What's wrong?" she asked. "Are
you hurt?"

"No," Sting replied, sighing. "But I'm
lost. It's my first time gathering pollen for

my hive, and I've worked hard all day.
Look!" She held up her back legs. Dazzle
could see that the fine hairs on them
were full of pollen. "Now I'm tired and I
want to go home," the bee went on, "but
I can't remember how to get back to my
hive. Plus, I'm loaded down with all this
pollen."

"We'll help you," Skipper said kindly,
hovering nearby. "Come on, fly with
us. Together, I'm sure we can get
you home."

Sting's face lit up. She tried to launch
herself into the air, but she was carrying
so much pollen that she could only fly for
a few seconds. The little bee plummeted
back down to the grass.

"I'm so tired," she explained. "I don't
know if I can fly anymore!"

"Tell you what," Twinkle said. "I'll zip around the meadow and see if I can spot any other bees. They'll be able to point out the way to your hive. Maybe they can even help you get back there." She shook her wings with a flourish. "I'm Twinkle, by the way, and these are my butterfly friends — Skipper, Dazzle, and Mallow," she said.

Sting waved a leg. "Hi," she said bashfully. "Thank you all for helping me."

"Here, Sting," Mallow called, landing on a nearby flower. The head of the flower dipped toward the bee. "Have some nectar while we wait for Twinkle to come back. It might give you more energy."

Sting smiled and sipped the nectar gratefully with her long tongue, while

17

Skipper and Dazzle used their wings to fan her. Dazzle exchanged an anxious glance with Skipper. She really hoped they could help the little bee get back home!

A few moments later, Twinkle returned. "Sorry, Sting," she said, landing next to the bee. "I looked all around the meadow. No bees. I asked a

couple of wasps and a gang of flies, but they hadn't seen your friends, either. It looks like they all went back to the hive."

Sting's smile faded. "I don't know what to do," she said. Tears welled in her eyes. "How will I get home now?"

Dazzle grabbed some soft, springy moss to dry Sting's tears. "Hey, it's OK," she said. "We'll help you get home. All you need to do is think hard about how you got to the meadow."

"That's the problem," Sting said. "I was so busy collecting pollen, I didn't watch where I was going. All I know is that I live in a hollow tree covered with honeysuckle . . . but I don't have a clue how to get back to it!"

CHAPTER FOUR

Into the Blue

"Once you've taken a rest, maybe you'll remember something if we all fly together," Skipper suggested to the little bee.

Mallow wiggled her antennae, then launched into a cheer:

"S — T — I — N — G

We will find that hollow tree!

One, two, three, four, five
Butterflies heading to the hive!"

Sting smiled at
Mallow's rhyme. "I do
feel a little better," she
said. "Thanks. Let's try
flying together."
She buzzed slowly
into the air, trying
hard to fly even though
she was weighed down.
The butterflies fluttered
up to join her, and they
set off around the
meadow.

"Does anything look
familiar?" Dazzle asked
hopefully as they passed
a patch of golden buttercups.

22

Sting gazed around, then shook her head. "Not really," she said. "But let's keep going. I don't want to give up!"

They flew on. "Do you recognize this big old tree?" Skipper asked a little while later, pointing it out with her wing.

"Well . . ." Sting started. She landed on a branch and looked around. Her wings slumped. "Oh, I'm all mixed up!"

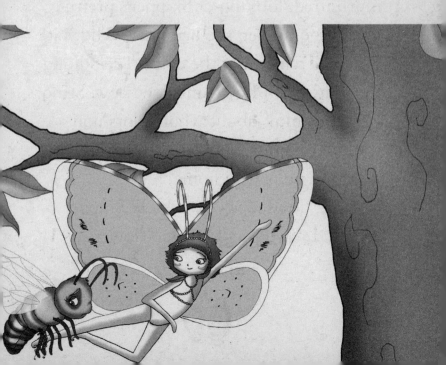

she exclaimed. "And I have to get all my pollen home. I was hoping the queen bee would be proud of me for collecting so much!"

"There must be something we can do," Skipper muttered. She sat next to Sting and fanned her wings, which sparkled in the sunshine.

"What a beautiful color," Twinkle murmured, looking at Skipper's pretty blue wings. Then she grinned. "That's it! I always remember the colors I see along the way when I go someplace new. Sting, can you think about what colors you spotted on your way here? It might help you find your way home!"

"Oh, good idea, Twinkle!" Skipper cried. "I always notice blue flowers,

especially if they're the same shade as my wings."

"I like yellow best," Dazzle said, fluttering her pale yellow wings proudly.

Mallow turned back to the honeybee. "Think hard, Sting," she urged. "Before you reached the meadow, what's the last color you remember seeing?"

Sting closed her eyes and was silent. Then her wings shook with excitement. "It's working!" she said. "I can remember seeing blue below me as I flew — blue, everywhere!"

Skipper flew loops in the air. "I know exactly where you were!" she cried. "Cornflower Valley. Follow me!" With a flash of her bright wings, she zoomed up and away.

CHAPTER FIVE

On the Path

Dazzle, Twinkle, Mallow, and Sting
took to the air behind Skipper. Sting was
flying much faster as they journeyed
across the meadow and all the way up
Juniper Hill.

Skipper paused at the top of the hill,
bobbing up and down excitedly. "Look,
look!" she cried as the others flew up

behind her. "There's blue *everywhere* down there."

Dazzle gazed down into the valley. Of course! A carpet of blue cornflowers stretched below them.

Sting buzzed with delight. "This is it!" she cried, beaming. "I was definitely here before. I remember!"

Skipper smiled. "I *thought* you might be talking about Cornflower Valley," she said happily. "It's one of my favorite places. So now we know you came into Butterfly Meadow from this direction."

But Sting
didn't seem to be
paying attention.
She was too busy
gazing at all the
beautiful
cornflowers.
"So many
flowers, so much
pollen to collect," she buzzed to herself.
Before the butterflies realized what was
happening, she went flying off toward
the blooms.

"Sting!" called Twinkle, darting
after her. "Stop! You can't collect more
pollen now."

"But I've got to get as much pollen as
I can," Sting replied, zooming down to
the first clump of cornflowers. "I want

the queen bee to see that I'm a good worker."

"You *are* a good worker, Sting. I'm sure the queen bee knows that," Dazzle told her. "But if you collect more pollen now, it will make you even heavier!"

"The sun will be setting soon," Mallow reminded the little bee. "We have to get you home before dark. Once the sun goes down, the colors will be harder to see."

Sting backed away from the cornflowers. "You're right," she said, sighing. "I just don't want to disappoint the queen bee. She's very grand, you know."

"Yes, we know," Skipper said. "We met her at Sports Day."

"She gave us each a touch of golden pollen on our wings," Mallow remembered, wriggling happily at the thought.

Twinkle clapped her wings together. "We need to keep moving," she reminded them all. "Sting, you did a great job remembering the cornflowers. What colors did you see before you got to Cornflower Valley?"

Sting thought hard. "I remember a circle of green," she said slowly. "It had white dots on it."

Dazzle looked around, confused. Where could this be? "Daisies in a field?" she guessed.

Sting shook her head. "I don't think so," she said. "The dots were bigger than daisies."

"Hmmm," Twinkle said. Nobody could come up with any other ideas! "Doesn't anybody know where this might be?"

If we can't solve this riddle, Dazzle thought, *we may never find Sting's home.*

CHAPTER SIX

Wake Up, Sting!

Suddenly, Mallow zipped high into the air, her antennae quivering. "Got it!" she exclaimed, whizzing back down to the others. "Sting, were the white dots near water?" she asked.

"Yes!" Sting cried, her eyes lighting up.

Mallow laughed. "The dots are water lilies," she explained to her butterfly

friends. "And the green
must be lily
pads. I think she's
talking about
Cowslip Pond!"
All the
butterflies
knew where
that was.
They had flown a relay race around
the pond during Sports Day. Plus, the
cool water was always refreshing on a
hot summer day.

"This way, Sting," Dazzle said, fluttering into the air again.

Dazzle led the colorful group through Cornflower Valley and on toward the pond. Once they arrived at the cool green water, the butterflies and Sting flew to rest in the shade of a leafy tree nearby.

"Phew," said Dazzle, sighing. She was hot and tired. Her wings ached, and she felt very thirsty. "Where now, Sting? Is it much farther?"

Sting let out a yawn. "I don't know," she admitted. "It's been a long

day, and being a worker bee is such . . .
hard . . . work. . . ."

Dazzle peered at Sting, wondering
why she was talking so slowly. Then
a tiny snore drifted through the
air. Dazzle saw that Sting's eyes were
closed.

"She fell asleep," Skipper said. "She
must be worn out, poor thing."

"She can't sleep now!" Twinkle cried.
"We have to get her back to the hive
before it gets dark."

"Sting? Sting!
Time to wake
up!" Mallow
called.
Sting didn't stir.
Dazzle plucked a

blade of grass and tickled the little bee's nose with it.

"Bzzzzzz . . ." Sting murmured sleepily, rubbing her nose and rolling over. She was still fast asleep!

Skipper waved a sweet-smelling white petal under Sting's nose. "This yummy smell will wake her up," she said.

Sure enough, Sting sniffed the air . . . but kept right on snoozing.

"S–T–I–N–G — wake up, little honeybee!" cheered Mallow. Not even that woke her!

The four butterflies looked at one another anxiously. "It'll be dark soon," Dazzle said. "We won't stand a chance of helping Sting get home if we can't see where we're going. But she's so sleepy. What can we do?"

CHAPTER SEVEN

A Helping Beak

Twinkle spread her wings wide. "I know who can help us," she said, sounding excited. "I'll be right back!"

Dazzle, Skipper, and Mallow watched her fly to the top of a tall, sturdy tree nearby. "What is she doing?" Skipper asked.

Mallow shook her head. "Who knows? Twinkle is always full of surprises."

"Look. She's coming back," Dazzle said as she spotted her friend's bright wings among the leaves.

"Who's that with her?" Skipper asked, peering into the sunny sky. A creature flew down next to Twinkle. It was much larger than a butterfly, but it was hard to tell exactly what it was with the sun shining in their eyes.

The creature let out a loud "ha-ha-ha!" noise, as if it were laughing. The butterflies all looked at one another, bewildered.

"It's a bird," Skipper said, as the creature drew closer. "Oh, it's beautiful — and as colorful as a butterfly!"

Dazzle stared at the new arrival. With its emerald-green back feathers, pale yellow underbelly, and crimson head, she had never seen such a colorful bird. But why was it laughing at them?

Twinkle landed next to her friends, followed by the bird, which bent its head in a polite bow.

"This is Boom — he's a woodpecker," Twinkle announced. "He's just what we need to wake Sting. Watch this!"

Boom perched on a branch close to the tree trunk and started tapping at the wood with his beak. *Drrr-rrrr-rrrr!* His sharp beak pecked away at the wood at record speed!

Dazzle could hardly think straight. The noise was so loud!

Sting's eyes snapped open and she looked around wildly. "Oh! What's happening?" she cried. "Who's knocking?"

Dazzle put out a comforting wing. "It's OK, Sting," she said. "Nobody's knocking — it's just Boom up there, see?"

Boom gazed down, his eyes merry and bright. "Just pecking for grubs," he called to Sting with a friendly wave of his green wing. His beak tapped against the wood so quickly, it became a blur.

"Now, Sting," Twinkle said loudly over Boom's pecking, "no falling asleep again. We need to get you home, remember?"

"What's our next color clue?" Mallow asked. "Can you

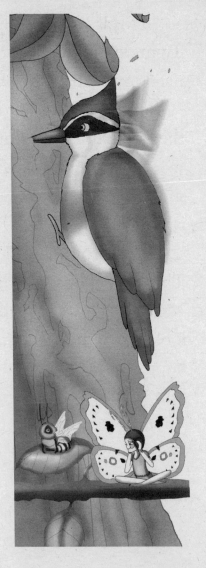

remember anything else that might help us find the way back to your hive?"

Sting thought for a moment, and shrugged her gauzy wings. "My hive is in a big, hollow tree that's covered with honeysuckle. The honeysuckle flowers just opened — they're creamy white and, boy, do they smell good."

"Hmmm," Skipper said. "I don't remember seeing that tree."

Dazzle shook her head. "Me, neither," she said.

Boom suddenly gave a cry. "Ha–ha–ha! I know that tree," he told them. "Hollow trees always make the

best sound. Your honeysuckle tree isn't far from here. Follow me." Boom spread his glossy wings and took off into the air.

"What are we waiting for?" Dazzle cried. "Let's go!"

She and her friends fluttered after the woodpecker. Dazzle had to flap her wings hard to keep up with the speedy bird. When she glanced back to check on Sting, she saw that the little bee was lagging behind. "Keep going, Sting," Dazzle urged.

Boom led them into a nearby forest. Sting suddenly let out a joyful shout. "Hey! I recognize this place," she cried. "I'm almost home!"

CHAPTER EIGHT

Home at Last

Dazzle thought Sting might burst with excitement! The little bee was buzzing loudly and flying quickly now, even though she still carried a lot of pollen.

A tall tree with a hole in its side loomed up ahead of them. White flowers bloomed on the honeysuckle plant that covered the trunk and branches of the tree.

"Oh, thank you!" Sting said, buzzing around in a circle. "It's so good to be back!"

"My pleasure, little buddy," Boom said. "Good-bye, everyone. Nice meeting you."

"Good-bye, Boom!" the butterflies and Sting called, waving their antennae as he flew away.

"Try the honeysuckle nectar," Sting urged the butterflies, flying to one of the white flowers. "It tastes so good."

The butterflies unrolled their long curled tongues to sip the sweet nectar. "Ahh, that's better," Skipper said after a long drink. "Thanks!"

"Let me show you my home," Sting said, buzzing up to the hive entrance. "If you peek in from here, you won't get honey on your wings. Come and see!"

Dazzle and her friends hovered
at the edge of the hive, peering inside.
The bees' nest looked waxy, and had
cells leading away from the central
open space. Two worker bees stood
guard at the entrance. Inside, lots
of other bees rushed around,
carrying nectar and pollen to feed
their young.

"Wow!" Mallow exclaimed. "It's so busy in there!"

"I can smell the honey," Dazzle said, breathing in the sweet air.

Sting bobbed up and down, looking proud of her fellow bees.

Just then, a large bee came out of one of the chambers and floated over to them. It was the queen bee! She had

thick, furry stripes on her body, and the most elegant buzz Dazzle had ever heard.

"There you are, Sting," the queen said. "We were so worried about you. Where have you been?"

Sting explained what had happened and told the queen bee how the butterflies had helped her find her way home.

"You did a wonderful job collecting so much pollen," the queen bee told her. "But you must be more careful next time. Stay with your friends, and don't stray too far from the hive."

Sting lowered her antennae and nodded. "Of course," she said.

The queen bee turned to the butterflies. "I'm so grateful to you for helping Sting," she said. "She's very important to us! Is there anything I can do to thank you?"

Twinkle dipped her wings and gave a little curtsy. "I've always wanted to taste honey," she said.

The queen bee smiled. "Then let's get you some!"

One of the worker bees flew over, carrying a sticky blob of honey between

her front legs.
She gave each
butterfly a
drop to try.

"Oooh,"
said Dazzle,
enjoying the
sticky sweetness.
"It's delicious."

"Thank you," Skipper said gratefully.
"What a treat!"

The queen bee glanced out of the
hollow. "It's getting dark," she said,
turning back to the butterflies. "Would
you like to stay here for the night?
There's plenty of room nearby, even if
you can't come into the hive."

"That's nice of you," Mallow
replied, "but our home is in Butterfly

Meadow. If we set off right away and fly fast, we'll be able to make it there by nightfall."

The queen bee nodded. "There's no place like home."

"Thanks again," Sting said to her new friends. "And good-bye. See you all again soon, I hope!"

Dazzle, Mallow, Skipper, and Twinkle all waved their wings before setting off for Butterfly Meadow.

Dazzle felt tired as the four friends fluttered away. "We flew a long way today," she said.

"We did," Mallow agreed. "But we made a new friend, helped her out, *and* tasted some delicious honey. All thanks to Twinkle, spotting Sting by the hedge."

Dazzle is at home in

Butterfly Meadow!

Here's a sneak peek at her next adventure,

Joy's Close Call!

❀ FUN FACTS! ❀
The Sweet Life of the Honeybee

Sometimes insects can cause trouble. Spiders spin sticky webs. Crickets make noise. Flies ruin picnics. But honeybees produce something sweet and good to eat — honey!

Almost no other insect works as hard as a honeybee. Honeybees work together to maintain their hive. Each hive has one queen and thousands of worker bees, and each bee has a job to do. Some clean or protect the hive. Others feed baby bees. Some collect nectar from flowers.

The nectar is stored in a honeycomb. Bees use their wings to dry the nectar, which leaves honey behind. One hive can produce more than 60 pounds of honey a year! Bees must collect nectar from millions of flowers to make one pound of honey. But honeybees don't mind sharing. They produce more honey than they need.

Bees can sting humans and animals to protect themselves and their hives. Each bee will sting only once. The stinger has a barb on the end that gets stuck in its victim. So watch out — don't annoy a bee!

CHAPTER ONE

A Surprise

"Hurry, Skipper!" Dazzle called. She watched the little blue butterfly swoop under the head of a daisy, then soar up to loop around the branch of an elm tree. "This could be your best time yet."

The two butterflies were having a great time flying through the obstacle course they had made in Butterfly

Meadow! Even the occasional raindrop wasn't enough to keep them from playing. Skipper skimmed over a crimson poppy and dashed toward the finish line. A friendly spider had spun them a finish line out of a thin silvery thread stretched between two tall clumps of grass.

"Good job, Skipper!" Dazzle cried, flying over to her friend. "You were much faster that time."

"I'm so hot," Skipper panted, flapping her wings. "Thank goodness for the rain shower. Even though I can't touch the raindrops, it's helping me cool down."

"I think the rain might stop soon." Dazzle glanced at the misty sky. "I can see the sun peeking through the clouds." As she watched, an arch of pale, beautiful colors appeared overhead, shimmering in the sunshine.

"Oh!" Dazzle gasped. "What's *that*, Skipper?"

Skipper turned to look. "I don't know," she breathed in awe. "I've never seen anything like it before."

"But where did it come from?" Dazzle wanted to know. Her gaze was fixed on the big, shining arch. "Look at all the different colors. I can see red, orange, and yellow —"

"And green, blue, indigo, and violet," Skipper added.

All the other butterflies in Butterfly Meadow had noticed the pretty arch, too. They were darting around, excited.

"Look! Isn't it *beautiful*?" Dazzle heard

her friend Mallow cry. She turned to see the cabbage white butterfly nearby.

"Mallow," Dazzle called, "do you know what that colorful ribbon is?"

"Of course," Mallow replied, twirling happily in the air. "It's a rainbow! It appears when rain and sunshine are mixed up together."

Dazzle and Skipper glanced at each other, grinning.

"Rainbow," Dazzle said softly. "What a pretty word."

"Hooray for the rainbow!" Mallow shouted, and all the butterflies cheered. "But now we have to hurry." Mallow turned to Dazzle, Skipper, and Twinkle. "Follow me!"

"Where are we going?" Dazzle

wondered aloud, as the three of them
fluttered after Mallow.

"I don't know," Skipper replied.
"Mallow, why are we in such a hurry?"

"Beauty, the oldest and wisest
butterfly in Butterfly Meadow, told me a
rainbow secret," Mallow answered. The
butterflies flew in closer. "She said that
rainbows lead to surprises! Something
special waits at the end of the rainbow."

Dazzle, Skipper, and Twinkle glanced
at one another in amazement.

"The rainbow began in Butterfly
Meadow, so now we have to track down
the other end of it to fine the surprise,"
Mallow said.

Dazzle couldn't wait!

Come flutter by Butterfly Meadow!

#1: Dazzle's First Day

#2: Twinkle Dives In

#3: Three Cheers for Mallo

#4: Skipper to the Rescue

#5: Dazzle's New Friend

#6: Twinkle and the Busy Be